Holiday HA-HA'S

Thanksgiving
Jokes + Riddles

LIBRARY O' LAUGHS

The author is thankful for
Donovan, Valissa,
Avarelle, Astrella, Alex

The illustrator is thankful for
Carole, Logan and Gabriel

Holiday HA-HA's
Thanksgiving
Jokes + Riddles

LIBRARY O' LAUGHS

PSS!
PRICE STERN SLOAN

These people aren't turkeys...

Jon Anderson, Kelli Chipponeri,
AnnMarie Harris, Clizia Gussoni,
Jaclyn Cozza, Jayne Antipow, Joy Court,
Luke McDonnell, Patricia Pasquale,
Rebecca Goldberg, Rosalie Lent

You know, I don't think turkeys would appreciate all the jokes I make about them in this book. And I'm pretty sure stuffing and pumpkin pies wouldn't find them amusing, either.

But luckily, I don't think turkeys, stuffing, or pumpkin pies can read, so as long as you don't go telling them any of these jokes, I should be safe.

So this Thanksgiving, if a turkey, a pumpkin pie, or some stuffing asks if you've heard any good jokes lately...you didn't hear them from me!

CRAIG

Craig Yoe

What did the Pilgrims have to clean
after the first Thanksgiving dinner?
-The Mess-achussetts!

What's cold and is in the
Thanksgiving Day Parade?
–Ice-cream floats!

What do basketball players say on Turkey Day?

—"Hoop-y Thanksgiving!"

What do you call the day after Thanksgiving?

—The day after Thanksgiving!

What do you sit on during Thanksgiving dinner?
—Your rump-kin pie!

What does an animated character say after Thanksgiving dinner?
-"I ate toon much!"

What does a 2,000 pound elephant eat on Thanksgiving?
—Ton-key!

Why doesn't a golfer want pumpkin pie on Thanksgiving?

-He doesn't like to have a slice!

What DOES a golfer like on Thanksgiving?

-Par-tatoes!

What November holiday does
a selfish person celebrate?
— Thanks-getting!

**Why don't turkeys like
Thanksgiving?**
—Because it's for the birds!

What did the Pilgrims eat during
their voyage to America?
— Fish 'n' ships!

What is in a genie's turkey?

—Three wishbones!

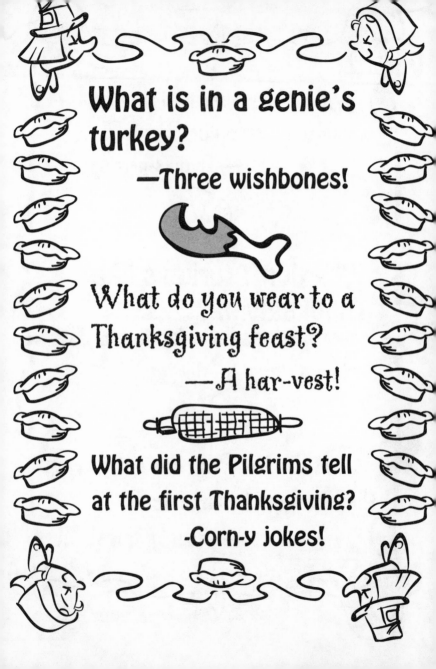

What do you wear to a Thanksgiving feast?

—A har-vest!

What did the Pilgrims tell at the first Thanksgiving?

-Corn-y jokes!

Peter Pan
+ Pumpkins

Peter Pie Pan

**What's the sleepiest thing
on the Thanksgiving table?
–The Nap–kins!**

What did Myles Standish
say after the first
Thanksgiving feast?

—"BURP!"

What does a Turkey pick out of his nose?

—A gobble-goober!

What is a football player's
favorite state?

—New Jersey!

Who has the least money at Thanksgiving?
–The poor-tatoes!

How can you recognize the turkey on Thanksgiving?
–He's the one in a fowl mood!

What do you say to a centipede at the Thanksgiving table?

—"Get your elbow, elbow off the table."

What does a butcher put under his plate at Thanksgiving dinner?
—A place-meat!

Why didn't the Pilgrims eat spaghetti at the first Thanksgiving?
—**They were anti-pasta!**

What's bigger, a football or a baseball?

    —Neither! They both have eight letters!

What do dogs wear when they play football?

        -Hel-mutts!

What would a British person gain if he ate a Thanksgiving dinner?

    -Pounds!

Burglar
+Turkey

"Robble, Robble!"

Why did the turkey cross the playground?

-To get to the other slide!

Which Thanksgiving food has grandchildren?

-The Gran-berry sauce!

What's black and white and red all over?
-An embarrassed Pilgrim!

Which hand should you butter a roll with at Thanksgiving dinner?
-Neither, you should use a knife!

Orange vegetable
+ Green vegetable
——————————
Pumpkin pea!

What kind of car does a Pilgrim drive?
  —A Mayflower Compact!

Why did the vegetables have to leave the Thanksgiving table?
    —They were fresh!

What did the mother turkey say to the baby turkey on Thanksgiving?
—"Don't gobble your food!"

What does a rapper like on Thanksgiving?
—Yo-tatoes!

What does Frosty the Snowman
eat on Thanksgiving?

   —Cold slaw!

What do you drink at
Thanksgiving dinner that
makes you burp?

   -Belch's grape juice!

What sound does a turkey
with a limp make?

   -"Hobble, hobble!"

When does a goldfish eat turkey?

—On Tanks-giving!

What does a road eat on Thanksgiving?

—Tar-key!

What does a small cake eat on Thanksgiving?
—Tart-key!

Why was the pig thrown out of the football game?
—Because he played dirty!

Who plays the music in outer space Thanksgiving Day Parades?
—Martian bands!

Where do you bury a potato from your Thanksgiving feast if it dies?

-In a grave-y!

What did the photographer say when he carved the turkey?

-"Watch the birdie!"

What band in the Thanksgiving Day Parade plays the bounciest music?

—The rubber band!

What did the tree say to the rake?

–"Leaf me alone!"

Which side of a turkey has the most feathers?

–The outside!

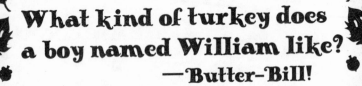

What kind of turkey does a boy named William like?
—Butter-Bill!

Which Pilgrim cut the turkey at the first Thanksgiving dinner?
—John Carver!

What does a mother present say to the kid present on Thanksgiving?

— "Keep your el-bows off the table!"

What does a scared person eat on Thanksgiving?

-Goosebump-kin pie!

What does a brainy girl say on Turkey Day?
—"Happy Thinks-giving!"

Why does a quarterback do so well in school?
—Because he always passes!

What do sandals say on Turkey Day?
-"Happy Thongs-giving!"

MAD ADD JOKE!

Corn
+ Turkey
───────────
"Cob-ble, cob-ble!"

Where does a quarterback go to dance on Saturday night?
—To the foot-ball!

Why didn't the turkey eat anything on Thanksgiving?
—He was stuffed!

What do you call a Thanksgiving dish that studies hard for a test?
—A cram-berry!

What was the Mayflower made out of?
—Wooden you like to know!

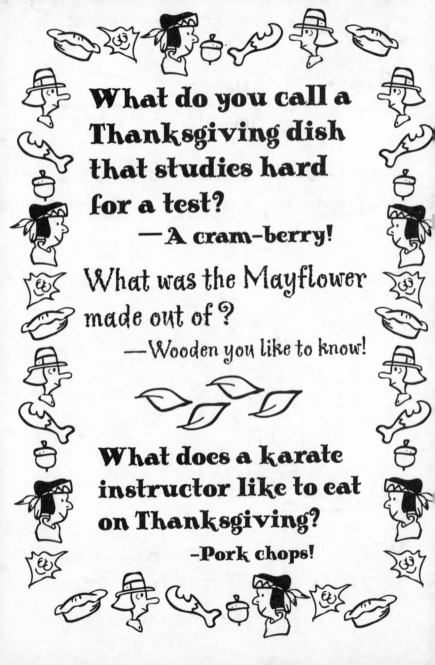

What does a karate instructor like to eat on Thanksgiving?
-Pork chops!

What does a dog put under his plate at Thanksgiving dinner?

—A place mutt!

What girl is always asked to say the blessing on Thanksgiving?

—Grace!

What does your mom say when she passes you the turkey?
-"Try this on for thighs!"

Why did the Pilgrim blush?
-He caught the turkey dressing!

How did the turkey get through Thanksgiving?
-He winged it!

What does an arithmetic teacher do at Thanksgiving?
-She counts her blessings !

Why did the Pilgrim
wash his hands before
Thanksgiving dinner?
    —To get rid of the pil-grime!

How many cranberries
grow on a bush?
    —All of them!

What does a gas station
attendant eat on
Thanksgiving?
        -Pump-kin pie!

Who flirted at the Thanksgiving table?
-The cranberry sauce-y!

Why did Dad save some of the turkey for tomorrow?
—He didn't want it to go to waist!

Why are you always full after eating pumpkin pie?

—Because of the fill-ing!

What does a turkey with two heads say?

—"Double, double!"

What do ghosts eat on Thanksgiving?

-Hot ghost-ed turkey!

What did the diamond eat on Thanksgiving?

–24 carrots!

What does a foot like on Thanksgiving?

–Pota-toes!

What does a computer eat on Thanksgiving?
        –A few megabytes!

Why did the Thanksgiving basket get in trouble at school?
    —Because it was caught cornu-copying!

What does a golfer like on Thanksgiving?
        —Putt-tatoes!

What does Godzilla like to eat at Thanksgiving?
-Squash!

On Thanksgiving, what's always in the middle of every table?

—The letter "B".

Thanksgiving dinner
+ Office message
_____
Turkey with all
the faxings!

**What class does a
turkey wrestle in?**
-Feather weight!

What football position does barbed wire play?
—De-fence!

On what holiday should you not take a cruise?
-Sanksgiving!

What advice did the speech teacher give the Thanksgiving pie?

-"Don't mince your words!"

What do Pilgrims use for a Thanksgiving centerpiece?

-May-flowers!

Why do you go to your Grandmother's house on Thanksgiving?

-Because the house won't come to you!

Which Thanksgiving beverage is sad?

–Apple sigh-der!

In what state did the Pilgrims first sneeze?

-Mass-ah-choo-setts!

What's the best thing to put in a pumpkin pie?
—Your teeth!

What does a fellow student eat on Thanksgiving?

-Peer-tatoes!

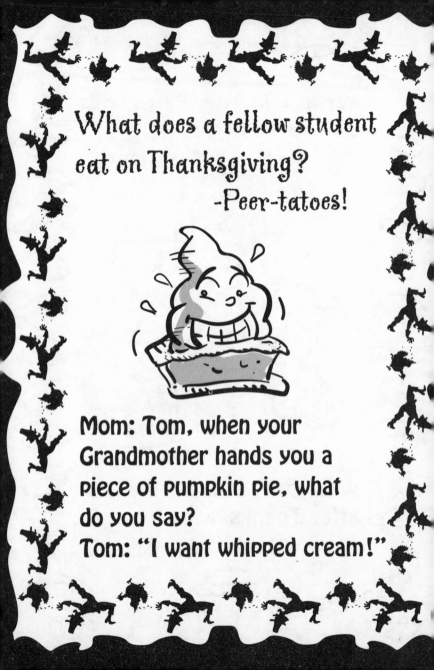

Mom: Tom, when your Grandmother hands you a piece of pumpkin pie, what do you say?

Tom: "I want whipped cream!"

What does a cat eat on Thanksgiving?

-Purr-tatoes!

What does a cow put under her plate at Thanksgiving dinner?

—A place moo-t!

What does a person who got hit in the head eat on Thanksgiving?
—Lump-kin pie!

What does a lobster put on his table before Thanksgiving dinner?
—A table claw-th!

What does a baby turkey say?
-"Goo-gooble, Goo-gooble!"

Which Thanksgiving food is the most courageous?
—The bravey!

How much does a turkey weigh?
—A few Pil-grams!

What's gross to put on potatoes?
—Butt-er!

What do police officers eat on Thanksgiving?
—Corn on the cop!

Which month is a flower's least favorite?

-No-stem-ber!

What does a baseball player put under his plate at Thanksgiving dinner?

-A place mitt!

MAD ADD JOKE!

Drum
+Thanksgiving Dinner
———————————————
Tom Tom Turkey

What's the best country to celebrate Thanksgiving in?
-Turkey!

What ship did the selfish
Pilgrims come to
America on?
—The Me-flower!

What did the kid look like after finishing his Thanksgiving desserts?

—Pie-eyed!

What does a pole-vaulter eat on Thanksgiving?
—Jump-kin pie!

Who would be at your Thanksgiving dinner if you celebrated it in the summer?
—Uncles and ants!

Which football game is played on Thanksgiving?
—The Gravey bowl!

What game do you play after eating too much turkey dinner?
-Moan-opoly!

Tom: I wish I were a Pilgrim!
Mom: Why?
Tom: Because then I wouldn't have to study them in history class!

Which month is a tailor's least favorite?
-No-hem-ber!

Why is Thanksgiving such a smart holiday?
-Because it's in Know-vember!

How do you say Happy Thanksgiving in French?

-"Happy Thanksgiving in French!"

What does a vulture say before Thanksgiving dinner?

—"Let us prey!"

What does a blackboard like to eat for Thanksgiving desert?
-Chalk-olate!

Which Thanksgiving vegetable can you get lost in?
-Maize !

What do cows eat on Turkey Day?
-A Thanksgiving moo-l!

Mom: Help me fix Thanksgiving dinner!
Tom: Why, is it broken?

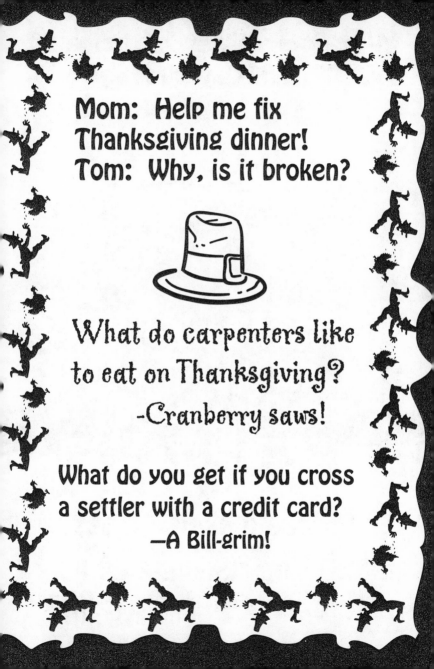

What do carpenters like to eat on Thanksgiving?
-Cranberry saws!

What do you get if you cross a settler with a credit card?
—A Bill-grim!

What does a horn eat on Thanksgiving?
—Toot-key!

What does a skeleton say before Thanksgiving dinner?
—"Bone appétit!"

Why does Thanksgiving have to be careful when it's walking?

—Because it always falls on Thursday!

What's the nicest vegetable at the Thanksgiving table?

—The sweet potato!

Where should you put the corn and carrots on Thanksgiving?

—On the vege-table!

Why couldn't Grandma find her napkin on the Thanksgiving dinner table?

-Because it was cran-buried!

What position does a mule play on a football team?
-Kicker!

MAD ADD JOKE!®

UFO
+ Thanksgiving fruit

Cranberry Saucer

What is a ballerina's favorite part of Thanksgiving?
-The cran-ballet sauce!

What does a turkey like to watch on TV?
—The Feather Channel!

Why is Thanksgiving such a forgetful holiday?
-Because it's in No-remember!

Knock, knock!
Who's there?
Justin!
Justin who?
Justin time for Thanksgiving dinner!

What's your father's favorite part of Thanksgiving?
-The pa-rade!

On which holiday should you eat a lot of hot dogs?

-Franks-giving!

What does an orchestra leader like to eat for Thanksgiving desert?

-Green cello!

On which holiday should you deposit all your money?
-Banksgiving!

What was the first thing the Pilgrims smelled when they got off the Mayflower?
-Plymouth Reek!

Which holiday is Henry's favorite?

-Hanksgiving!

Which bugs aren't welcome at Thanksgiving dinner?

-Thanksgiving fleas-t!

What does a turkey say
before Thanksgiving dinner
and you say afterward?
-"I'm stuffed!"

What do flower children
say on Turkey day?
-"Hippy Thanksgiving!"

Who comes to a napkin's Thanksgiving meal?
-Nap-kin folk!

How much do Pilgrims' shoes cost?
-A Buckle!

What's a cat's favorite part of Thanksgiving?
-The purr-ade!

Knock, knock!
Who's there?
Bern!
Bern, who?
Bern the turkey? I can smell it from here!

Why don't turkeys make good baseball players?

–They hit a lot of fowl balls!

What kind of car does a Pilgrim like?

—A Pilgrim thinks a Plymouth rocks!

How far did the Pilgrims travel to come to America?

-3,000 Myles Standish!

What kind of sickness can you only get on Thanksgiving?
—Turkey pox!

What Thanksgiving vegetables can lift a lot of weight?
—Strong beans!

What do you call a place that only hires turkeys?
—Turkey staffing!

Mom: Would you like more vegetables?

Tom: No thanks, I don't carrot for them!

What did one raw vegetable say to the other at Thanksgiving dinner?

-"Let's go for a dip!"

**What is a genie's favorite part
of a Thanksgiving turkey?**

-The wish-bone!

$$\frac{\text{Dizzy person} + \text{Turkey}}{\text{"Wobble, Wobble!"}}$$

What's the most boring thing on the Thanksgiving table?
-The can-dulls!

What does Santa Claus
eat on Thanksgiving?
      -Turkey, what else?

**What do optimists say
on Turkey Day?**
   –"Hope–y Thanksgiving!"

How do you feel after eating
a huge Thanksgiving meal?
      —Very thank-full!

What kind of swimming does a turkey do?
—The turkey breast stroke!

Who was the snobbiest person at the first Thanksgiving?
-Myles Stand-offish!

What did the pilgrims sail on to come to the first Thanksgiving dinner?

-A gravy boat!

What does a can eat on Thanksgiving?
—Tin-key!

What did the mother cranberry say to the kid cranberry?
—"Don't sauce me!"

Who is always sad at Thanksgiving?
-A Pil-grim!

What kind of vision did the Pilgrims have? —16/20!

What does a camel eat on Thanksgiving?
-Hump-kin pie!

What section does the head of a football team sit in on an airplane?
—Coach!

What do you put on when you eat Thanksgiving dinner?
—Weight!

What is the saddest thing you can put on pumpkin pie?
–Weeping cream!

What do plumbers like to eat on Thanksgiving?
–Pumpkin pipe!

Why are pumpkin pies obnoxious?

-They have a lot of crust!

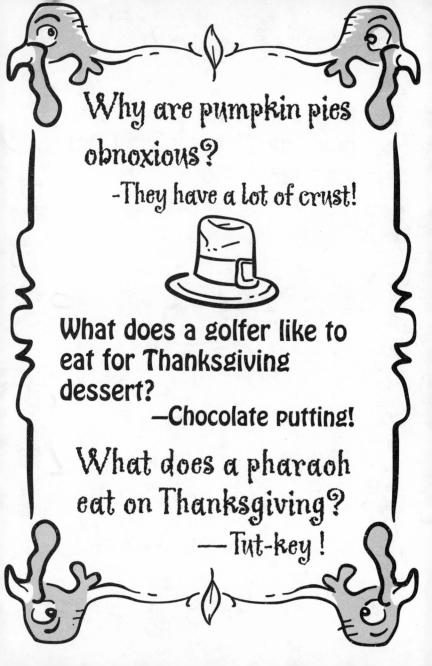

What does a golfer like to eat for Thanksgiving dessert?

—Chocolate putting!

What does a pharaoh eat on Thanksgiving?

—Tut-key!

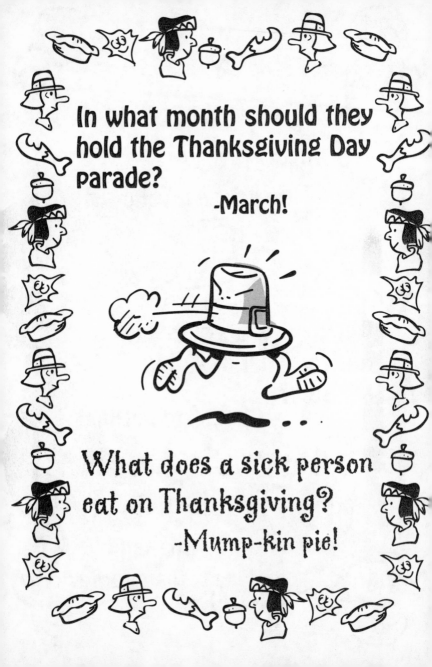

In what month should they hold the Thanksgiving Day parade?

-March!

What does a sick person eat on Thanksgiving?

-Mump-kin pie!

What does a doorknob eat on Thanksgiving?
-A turn-key!

What do Martians eat their turkey on?
-Flying saucers!

Why don't you eat fish on Thanksgiving?
-Because Thanksgiving never falls on Fry-day!

Loon: How many people does it take to stuff a turkey?
Goon: I don't know, I've never stuffed a turkey with people before!

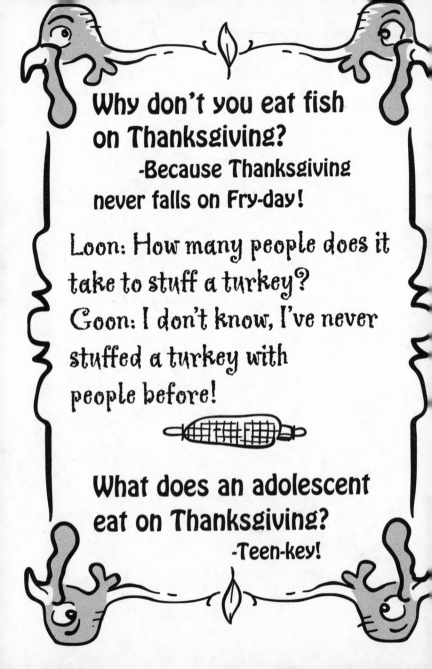

What does an adolescent eat on Thanksgiving?
-Teen-key!

What is a vampire's favorite holiday?
–Fangs–giving!

Which vegetable do rich people eat on Thanksgiving?
-14 karats!

What kind of turkey does a cow eat?
-Butter-bull!

What do you say to start a conversation during Thanksgiving dinner?

-"Let's talk turkey!"

Why was Plymouth Rock so brave?

—Because it was a little bold-er!

Which football team pays one dollar for corn?
-The Buck-an-ears!

What does a police officer put on his Thanksgiving table?

-A corny-cop-ia!

Where did the Pilgrim put her first bite of turkey?
-In her Ply-mouth!

Why do bakers make pumpkin pie?
-They knead the dough!

What does a hippie put on his potatoes on Thanksgiving?
-Groovy!

What does a doe say during Thanksgiving dinner?
-"This is deer-licious!"

What does a cactus eat after Thanksgiving dinner?

-Desert!

What sound does a turkey who steals things make?

-"Robble, robble!"

Why did the turkey play drums in the band?

--He had the drumsticks!

What ship did the Pilgrims' mothers come to America on?
-The Ma-flower!

What do beatniks say on Turkey day?
–"Hep–py Thanksgiving!"

What do you call an ache in your side after eating Thanksgiving dinner?
—A cramp-berry!

Why was the butter successful on Thanksgiving?

-He was on a roll!

What do rabbits say on Turkey Day?

-"Hop-py Thanksgiving!"

Why is Thanksgiving a lot like Halloween?

-Because it's in Novampire!

What's the best thing to have on top of a piece of pumpkin pie?

—Another piece of pumpkin pie!

How much did the
Mayflower weigh?
A puri-ton!

Why is the weather so
cold on Thanksgiving?
-Because it's Novem-brrrr!

Where did the pig go for Thanksgiving vacation?
—Boar-muda!

What do you eat a very small piece of pumpkin pie with?
–Sliver-ware!

What did the trumpet say after Thanksgiving dinner?
-"I ate toot much!"

How does a pie feel if it falls off the table?
-Crumb-y!

What do you call potatoes that fall on the floor at Thanksgiving dinner?
-Smashed potatoes!

What did the knife and spoon sing to the other piece of silverware?

—"Fork he's a jolly good fellow!"

What does a garbage collector eat on Thanksgiving?

-Dump-kin pie!

What sound does a turkey's phone make?
— "Wing, wing!"

What Thanksgiving vegetable flattens everything you put it on?
— Squash!

What does a ship eat on Thanksgiving?
— Pier-tatoes!

Why didn't anyone like the baked potatoes at Thanksgiving dinner?
-Because they were dud spuds!

What do angels say on Turkey Day?
-"Harp-y Thanksgiving!"

What is ice cream's favorite part of Thanksgiving?

-All the floats in the parade!

Why do so many people get hurt at Thanksgiving time?

-Because it's in the fall!

What is the nicest dish at Thanksgiving dinner?

—The sweet peas!

On which holiday should you play a lot of jokes on people?

-Pranks-giving!

What does the ocean like to put on its turkey?

-Wave-y!

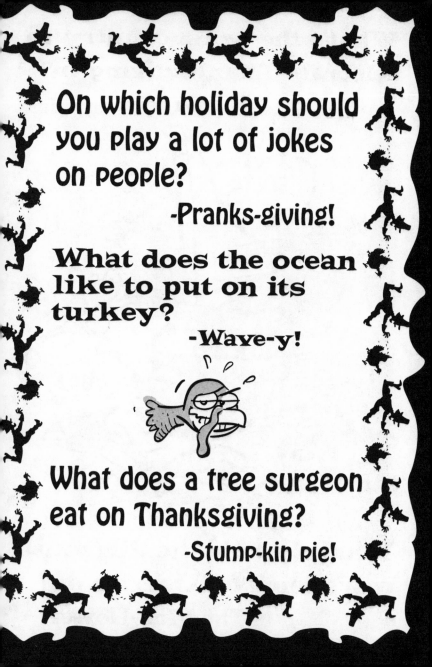

What does a tree surgeon eat on Thanksgiving?

-Stump-kin pie!

What's the worst country to celebrate Thanksgiving in?
-Greece!

What ship did the **Pilgrims'** cows come to America on?
-The Moo-flower!

What did the Pilgrims use to till the soil?
-A Plymouth rake!

Why do you drink so much water on Thanksgiving?

-Because it's always celebrated on Thirst-day!

What does a lifeguard say at Thanksgiving dinner?

-"Can I have another HELP-HELPING?!"

Why did the turkey get thrown out of the basketball game?
-He had too many fowls!

Why was the turkey feeling down?
-Because he had a lot of feathers!

Why did the turkey cross the road?
–It was the chicken's day off!

What do monsters have on their Thanksgiving table?
-Knives, forks and goons!

What did the early settlers take when they were sick?
—Pill-grims!

What do you pay for
your turkey dinner?
    -A Thanksgiving fee-st!

Why are so many new
cars sold around
Thanksgiving?
        -It's a good time to buy
an autumn-mobile!

What does a king put
under his plate at
Thanksgiving dinner?
        -A place-moat!

What is big and green and goes "gobble gobble"?

-Turkeysaurus Rex!

What item on a Thanksgiving table has a lot of energy?

-The pep-per!

Where did the Pilgrims throw their trash after dinner?

-In the Mayflower Compactor!

Why do turkeys like to play badminton?

-Because you play with birdies!

What does a wrench eat on Thanksgiving?

—Torque-y!

Why should your dinner table have four equal sides on Thanksgiving?

—So you can eat a square meal!

What Thanksgiving vegetable can you use to tie your shoes?
—String beans!

What kind of music shouldn't you play around the Thanksgiving Day Parade balloons?

—Pop!